D0049521

THE NO-DOGS-ALLOWED RULE

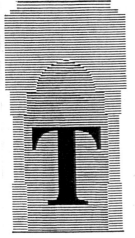

THE NO-DOGS-ALLOWED RULE

J
FICTION
Sheth

BY KASHMIRA SHETH

ILLUSTRATED BY CARL PEARCE

ALBERT WHITMAN & COMPANY
CHICAGO, ILLINOIS

Library of Congress Cataloging-in-Publication Data

Sheth, Kashmira.
The no dogs allowed rule / by Kashmira Sheth ;
illustrated by Carl Pearce.
p. cm.
Summary: Third-grader Ishan Mehra wants his family
to get a dog, but his efforts to convince his parents
often get him into trouble.
ISBN 978-0-8075-5694-8 (hardcover)
[1. Dogs—Fiction. 2. East Indian Americans—Fiction.]
I. Pearce, Carl, ill. II. Title.
PZ7.S5543No 2012
[E]—dc23
2011036689

10 9 8 7 6 5 4 3 2 1 LB 16 15 14 13 12

For more information about Albert Whitman & Company, visit our
Web site at www.albertwhitman.com.

For Leela with love.

ONE

"Eeeee . . . shaaaan," my brother yells.

When Sunil is annoyed, he stretches my name. "I'm riiiiiight heeeeere," I say.

Sunil frowns. His eyebrows look like two fuzzy caterpillars stuck on his round face.

He points to the Please Knock sign on his door. "Follow the rule."

Sunil's a fourth grader. Maybe in fourth grade they teach you how to turn into a rule-loving super-bore. Yikes! I'm in trouble, because that's where I'll be going next year.

Today I need Sunil's help, so I walk out and close the door. I knock. "Ishan Mehra."

"Arragh!" Sunil says.

I high-five the door open. "Listen," I say.

"Don't want to," Sunil grumbles.

"Fine, don't. But then you can't play with the dog."

He turns over. "We don't have one."

"We'll have a dog soon."

I want a dog as badly as a dog wants a treat. So does Sunil—not the dog treat, just the dog.

I think. You never know with Sunil though.

I pull his blanket off. "Don't be a lazy caterpillar in a cocoon. We need to ask for a dog. Now."

Sunil's face scrunches. I can't tell if he's mad or if he can't see me clearly.

I hand him his glasses from the nightstand. He puts them on. "Why?"

"Because summer break will start in four weeks, and we've got to get a puppy! Plus this is a long weekend, and Mom isn't on call." Our mom is a doctor and sometimes works on weekends. She takes care of babies: crying babies, pooping babies, sick babies, and us, even though we're not babies.

Sunil sits up on his bed. "What's your plan?"

"To beg and bug Mom and Dad until we get a dog."

"It won't work." He lies back down, pulls up his blanket, and picks up a book.

"Be lazy and stay in your cocoon," I say.

"Hey, you haven't hidden a cocoon in my room, have you? Like you hid that grasshopper?"

"If I hide, I don't tell."

Before he jumps up and grabs me, I dash to my room.

On my door hangs a sign. It's wild and

colorful with bugs drawn on it. I tried gluing a real dead Chinese beetle, but it wouldn't stick.

Anyway, on my painting it also says, "Home of Creepy Crawly Slimy Creatures and Ishan."

My name is spelled Ishan and is pronounced *E-shan*. It's not a weird name and I'm not a weirdo. Even though I was born and live in Oshkosh, Wisconsin, I have an Indian name. It's because my parents came from India a long time ago. That's why they gave my brother and me nice Indian names, even though he *is* a weirdo.

While I change my clothes, I decide to go solo and ask for a dog all by my lonely self. I slide down the banister because that way the steps don't squeak and wake up Mom and Dad. Luckily, I'm the only one who uses the banister, so it's not worn out. Not yet.

I tiptoe past Mom and Dad's room and wander into the kitchen. The stainless-steel container with round *laddus* is on the island. The sweet *laddu* is full of almonds and almonds are good for your brain. That's what Mom says. Maybe eating *laddu* will help me come up with a great dog-getting idea, so I help myself to one.

TWO

I TAKE A BITE OF *LADDU* AND THINK.
We have a no-dogs-allowed rule.
It's a no-fair and no-fun rule.

The only way I can get a puppy is if Mom changes the rule. She's the alpha dog of our pack.

It means she's the boss of our family. She bosses Sunil and me. "Pick up your toys," she'll say. "Clean up the table. Take a shower." She even bosses Dad. "Don't forget to get the groceries," and, "You better fix that wobbly chair."

So I decide to cook Mom breakfast to make her happy. Maybe then she'll change her mind.

Mom likes potato-stuffed bread. So I log on to the computer and type *paratha*.

Many sites pop up. I click on an *aloo paratha* recipe because *aloo* means *potatoes* in Hindi.

First it says:

BOIL FIVE MEDIUM POTATOES.

MAKE DOUGH WITH WHOLE-WHEAT FLOUR.

The rest of the recipe is long—like something Sunil would write. He didn't write it. He would never cook because he likes everything sparkly clean. I don't mind messy because I'm an artist.

I stop reading and get going. Usually, I'm not allowed to use the stove unless Mom and Dad are with me. But today is *un*usually, which means it is not usually. So I think it's okay to use the stove by myself. Plus, Mom and Dad are just around the corner in their room so they're

kind of with me. Plus, *plus*, I'm going to be very careful so there shouldn't be any problem.

I put water in a pot and plop five potatoes in. I turn on the stove.

Then I take a mixing bowl, open the pantry, and dump some flour in the bowl. The whole-wheat flour is the color of my skin. There're three more containers with flour: white, yellow, and dark gray. Mom uses the white one to make *naan* and the yellow one to make fried *pakoras*. I don't know what she uses the gray one for, but she must use it for some Indian food.

I dump some of each of them in the mixing bowl, too. That way my *parathas* will be like the multigrain bread we buy at the store.

Sometimes Mom makes a well in the pile of flour, adds oil, and covers it up. Then she lets me find the oil well. I make a well by scooping some of the flour to the side. The well is deep because it takes a quarter of a bottle of oil to fill up. I don't have time to play today so I don't go looking for the oil well.

I'm responsible like that.

I mix the oil and flour. Some of the mixture spills out, so I dump all of it on the counter.

Still, I can't knead it. The mixture and I are having problems.

When Sunil and I fight, Mom tells us to leave each other alone. So I leave the mixture alone.

I set the table. Mom usually decorates the table with flowers or colorful leaves. She likes to bring nature in. So I head out with the garden scissors.

The driveway is wet and covered with earthworms. I've got to move them before they get crushed under our car. I pick them up, hang ten of them onto my wrists, and drop them in soil. While I'm taking care of the last few of the driveway earthworms, "Boo!" Someone tries to scare me.

It's Jenna!

She is seven and lives right across from us.

Sunil thinks she likes me. Yikes! "When did you sneak up on me?" I ask.

She giggles. There's a big gap in her mouth because she's missing some teeth.

"What're you doing?" she asks.

I pick an earthworm from my wrist and hang it on her wrist. That way she knows what exactly I'm doing.

Her freckled face turns sickly. "Yuck. Take away your stupid, slimy worm!" she screams. She shakes her hand until it drops.

"Earthworms aren't stupid. They're good for the soil," I tell her.

"My uncle is an entomologist. That means he knows all about insects and bugs."

"But you don't."

"I do, too." She sticks out her tongue. Then she runs away.

I cut peonies and hurry back inside before Jenna returns.

I stand the peonies in a watering can and

set it on the table. They're so fresh they aren't open yet, and ants are chasing one another up and down the watering can. Mom likes flowers and I like ants. Both are nature.

They make a very *lively* arrangement.

Click-clank-bang. Mom's up. Yikes!

I poke a fork in one of the potatoes. The potato doesn't bounce back. That means they are done. I turn off the stove.

To cool the potatoes, I drop tons of ice

cubes in the pot. Then I mash them.

The fifth step of the recipe says, "Add red pepper, three cloves of crushed garlic, ginger salt, and—"

I open the spice cabinet. It's like a spice zoo! No time to read the labels.

One by one, I open each bottle, hold it upside down over the mashed potatoes, and shake it three times. I take three garlic cloves. I don't know what Mom uses to smash garlic. Sunil's pencil box is sitting on top of his backpack. It's a metal one so it works great. I throw the smooshed garlic into the potatoes.

Phew! Now Sunil's pencil box stinks.

I toss a fistful of salt and pour some lemon juice onto the mashed potatoes.

I stir them up. When I try the mixture, my mouth puckers, my nose wrinkles, and my teeth chatter.

I hear Mom turn off the shower. Double yikes!

THREE

I'M GOOD AT MIXING COLORS. I bet I'm good at mixing food, too.

"Hey Flour-and-Oil, meet Spice-Potatoes." I introduce them. Then I jumble them until they turn into a huge blob.

I heat up a skillet, drop some of the mixture on it, and spread it around.

It sizzles.

I wait for it to cook. I don't know how to tell when one side is done, so I let it cook and cook. It's better to overcook than undercook because that way it won't taste doughy and limpy.

"What's that smell?" Mom asks as she walks in.
I give her a hug. "Surprise! *Aloo paratha!*"
She looks around the kitchen. Her mouth twitches. She cranes her neck. "The smoke!"

16

"Oops!" I run back to the stove and flip the
paratha over.

The smoke detector goes off. *TEEEEEEEE.*

Dad rushes in with a toothbrush in his mouth.

17

The rule in our family is, if the smoke detector goes off, we've got to get out and wait on the sidewalk. Sunil runs down the steps holding on to his glasses.

I wave. "False alarm."

As always, Sunil ignores me. He dashes out the front door.

In his Wimpy Kid pajamas.

Dad opens the windows. "What did you do, Ishan?" He sprays foam as he talks. I'm not for more rules, but there should be one against spraying foamy toothpaste.

The alarm stops ringing.

"I was making *paratha* to surprise Mom and make her happy so she . . ."

Oops—I almost gave away my secret.

"So she what?"

"So she's very, very happy."

"Hmmm! We'll talk. After I finish brushing," he says.

I'm not fond of "talks" that end in me

getting a time-out.

The front door bangs open. Sunil hobbles in. It must be his new style of barefoot hop-hopping.

"What happened to your foot?" Mom asks.

"A dead earthworm is stuck to the bottom of my foot!"

"I must've missed that poor earthworm when I was moving the worms from the driveway to the garden," I say. "Why did you smoosh him?"

"I didn't do it on purpose. You . . . you made me run out barefoot. And kill the earthworm. You wait, Ishan, I'm going to get you."

"Don't you want to get rid of that dead body sticking to your foot first?" I ask.

He hobbles up the stairs looking red and mad.

Mom plops down on a chair and holds her head in her hands.

"Do you have a headache?" I ask.

"Yes."

I wonder what gave her a headache. "Eat some breakfast."

She looks up. Her eyes get larger and larger, like peonies opening up. She points at the watering can full of flowers.

"Don't you like flowers, Mom?"

"Not with the ants."

"Please move your party outdoors," I say to the ants. I pick up the *lively* flower arrangement and carry it outside.

I bring the *paratha*, with the burned side on the bottom, to Mom. When we go to an Indian restaurant, Mom asks for crispy *paratha*. Burned *paratha* are extra, extra super crispy.

"Close your eyes, please," I tell her.

I slip a bite of *paratha* into her mouth. She scrunches her nose and squints her eyes.

She doesn't spit! "It's garlicky and lemony and—"

"Extra crispy. You love it!"

"I—I don't—"

Darn! "You hate it?" I droop like a busted balloon.

I make puppy eyes.

Mom pulls me closer. "Let's add more flour. It'll taste delicious."

"You're the best, Mom." I give her a hug because she deserves one. *Deserve* means when someone does something to make you happy, and so you want to do something to make them happy.

FOUR

I ADD MORE FLOUR AND KNEAD THE MIXTURE. I pinch off a bit and roll it out. Mom cooks it. We keep on rolling and cooking, again and again. By the time Dad makes the tea, we have a stack of *parathas*.

Sunil comes down. He's never in the kitchen except when we sit down to eat. Then he appears magically.

He's changed into regular clothes. About time.

"These aren't *parathas*," Sunil says with a guppy face. It's the opposite of a happy face.

"What are they? Frisbees?" I ask.

He picks up his pencil box. "It stinks of garlic!" He lunges toward me. "I'm, I'm going to—"

Dad puts his arm out. "No fights."

Sunil washes his pencil box and then fixes himself a bowl of cereal.

Bor-ing!

"Excuse me, I want to organize the garage before I take a shower," Dad says, taking his empty dishes to the sink.

Hmmm! He has forgotten about the "talk."

Mom is reading a newspaper and enjoying her breakfast.

"Is your headache gone?" I ask her.

"Yes! Thanks for making the delicious *parathas*."

"Aren't they the best thing you've ever eaten?"

Her eyes turn beady. "What do you want?" she asks, just like that.

I don't know *why* she thinks I want something. But now that she asks I have to tell her. I cross my fingers for extra luck. The fingers slide over each other because they are a little *paratha*-greasy. "Mom, can we get a puppy to play with?"

"You have a brother to play with. You don't need a puppy."

"Alex has a sister and a brother. And they have dogs," I say. Alex is my best friend. He has two dogs, Toby and Sally, and a cat, Tiger. I don't mention Tiger because he reminds me of a real tiger. "All I want is one puppy. Please?" I make my voice extrasweet and my face extrasad.

Mom shakes her head. "No"

"I told you so!" Sunil says.

Whose side is Sunil on? "You want a puppy, too!" I yell.

Mom moves her finger across her mouth, which means I should be *choop*. *Choop* means *quiet*.

I shove a big piece of *paratha* into my mouth.

I think while I chew because I have to be *choop*.

Just then, Sunil says, "Ishan, I bet you don't know what five times five is." Sunil thinks he's smarter than me.

I SO DO NOT think so.

I reply, "Ysh hi *duh* thow," which in a non-chewing voice means, "Yes, I *do* know."

"What?" Sunil asks.

When I open my mouth again, a gob of half-chewed food gets away, hits the edge of the table, and lands on Sunil's lap.

"Gross!" he yells as he gets up. Unluckily, the blob hits Mom's bare foot and drops on the floor.

Mom's face gets monster-y. "Ishan Mehra!

Keep the food where it belongs."

"Sorry!" I take my paper napkin and bend down. I pick up the blob and stick it on Sunil's pants when he's not looking.

Mom looks at my crumpled napkin. "Good," she says. She must think I picked up the blob. "I'm going to the grocery store now. You both behave."

As soon as Mom leaves, Sunil gets up from his chair. The blob gets unstuck, rolls forward, and drops on the floor. Sunil steps on it. "Gross!" He picks up his leg like a dog ready to pee. "What's that?"

"A smooshed jellyfish," I say.

His eyes become beady like Mom's. "I bet you stuck that on me. Show me that napkin."

I grab my napkin. As quick as a grasshopper, I take off.

"I'll get you!" Sunil shouts.

"Wipe your feet first. If you make a mess, Mom will get mad."

"Arragh!"

I rush into the bathroom and lock the door. I flush the napkin down the toilet.

I'm quick like that.

Sunil knocks on the door. *Bang, bang.*

"Hey Sunil, that jellyfish probably hitchhiked on a boat from the ocean to Lake Michigan. Then it found its way here," I say.

No answer.

I open the bathroom door a crack. Sunil's

crazy face is there. Yikes!

He kick-opens the door.

He snoops in the wastebasket, bathtub, and under the sink. "Where's the napkin?" he roars. The toilet stops humming. "You flushed it?"

I cross my hands over my chest. "I'm being *choop*," I say. That way I don't have to answer him.

He grabs my hands and pins them to the wall. "I'm going to turn you into a jellyfish."

I press my lips tight.

His grip gets tighter. "Talk."

"Yeeeeees, I flushed it," I yelp, turning from *choop* to un-*choop*.

"Wait till I tell Mom," he says. He lets my hands go.

"Then we won't get a puppy. You want that?" I shove him.

Sunil looks puzzled. He can't figure out what he wants—to complain to Mom or to get a dog.

"Let's ask Dad for a puppy," I tell Sunil while

he's unpuzzling himself. Dad is the beta dog of our family. He's a second boss. He also bosses us: "Be quiet, let Mom rest, don't fight."

Sunil washes his hand because he touched the garbage can and me. "Dad won't say yes."

"When we beg, Dad buys us treats. Mom never does. You should ask him for a dog."

"Why me?"

"I asked Mom. It's your turn to ask."

He wipes his hands. "Okay."

I don't think Sunil's going to tell Mom about the blob.

FIVE

DAD IS ORGANIZING THE GARAGE. He shoves my red sleigh way back on the shelf. I better remember it because by next winter, Dad will forget where he organized it.

"Dad, can we get a dog?" Sunil asks.

"How about a fish?"

"A fish can't go for a walk or fetch a stick," Sunil says.

I give him a clown-smile, big and wide.

"And it can't give sloppy kisses, jump, or bark," I say.

"I don't need sloppy kisses. And we have enough jumping with you two around," Dad says.

"What about the bark?" I ask.

"No bark, no dog."

Most of the time I like Mom and Dad very much. But right now I'm not a big fan of them or the word *no*.

Sunil shakes his head. "I'm going to practice my violin." He goes back into the house.

"I don't feel good, Dad," I say.

"Let's go in so you can lie down."

I rest on the sofa. Dad kneels down by me. "Where does it hurt?"

"All over. If we get a dog, I'll feel better."

"Hmmm! You have Canine Deficiency Syndrome, CDS."

"Is CDS bad?"

"Nope. A cookie or a *laddu* will take care of it."

Dad knows I love cookies and sweet Indian

laddu. But I shake my head. "All I want is a puppy."

Dad pats me on the head. "Mom doesn't want one."

I sit up. "But if Mom wanted one, then would you want one?"

"Right now I'm dusty and sweaty. I want to take a shower and then do my research." Once Dad gets going on his research, he won't have time to talk dog.

The only way I can stop Dad's research is by hiding all three pairs of his glasses. He usually wears his black pair. I look on his desk, on the coffee table, and even in the cracks between the couch cushions. They aren't there.

I run to Dad's room, where he keeps the silver pair. They're inside a case on his nightstand.

I drop them in Sunil's underwear drawer. I'm careful not to touch anything in there.

The red pair isn't in Dad's closet, in his

drawers, or in his coat pockets. The only place
I don't look is in his bathroom because he's
in there. I'm so tired by all the looking that I
lie down on the carpet. And then I see them.
Dad's glasses are hanging out with dust bunnies
under the bed.

I pull them out, wash them, wipe them with
my shirt, and stick them in a pansy pot. Pansies
are colorful flowers that look like faces, and

Dad's glasses have a colorful trim, so they kind of go together.

By the time Dad's done showering, I'm back couching.

Oh no! He's holding his glasses—the black pair he was wearing.

"Dad, can you get me some water?" I ask.

He puts his glasses on the desk next to his computer and goes into the kitchen. I leap up and grab them. There's a statue of Buddha with his eyes half-closed on the fireplace. Quickly, I put the glasses on him and plop back on the couch.

Dad hands me a glass of water. "Feel better?"

"Yes. Thanks."

"Let me get some work done. When Mom comes, we can talk about getting a dog," he says.

I'm so happy, I need ten faces like Ravana to fit my smile. "Sure."

"My glasses were right here," Dad mumbles as he looks under the table, on the shelf, even in the bathroom—but not at the Buddha. "I'll get my spare pair."

Yikes! I wish I hadn't hidden his glasses.

Dad comes back, scratching his head.

"Where are my glasses, young man?" he asks, just like that.

Sunil is older, so you would think Dad would ask Sunil first. "What if Sunil hid them?" I shrug as if I'm just taking a guess. "Like in his underwear drawer?"

He goes upstairs to Sunil's room. I lie back on the couch and close my eyes.

"Dad!" Suddenly, Sunil's outer-space voice comes on. Outer-space voice is way louder than playground voice, even. "Why would I hide your glasses in my underwear drawer? I bet it was Ishan."

Dad marches down the stairs. "Young man, where's the other pair?"

I open my eyes just a crack. "Did you check the pansy pot?"

When Dad goes to check out the pansy pots, Sunil thunders down. "You're in big trouble, Ishan."

He makes a fist, but just then, Dad walks back, twirling his red glasses. "These are my favorite pair, Ishan. Thanks for finding them."

Sunil's fist goes limp.

I smile. "You're welcome, Dad."

Sunil looks sour, like stale barf.

He stomps up the stairs.

Dad's so happy with his red pair of glasses that he doesn't ask for the pair he was wearing.

Buddha looks sharp and smart with glasses. Maybe he'll get to keep them.

Dad sits down at his computer.

"Dad, if *search* is to look, then *research* is to look again, right?" I ask.

"I suppose." He taps his feet to a Hindi song.

When Dad says, "I suppose," it means he's not sure.

"Maybe someone searched it and then hid it. Now you have to re-search it," I say.

Dad strokes his imaginary beard. "I suppose."

He isn't sure, so I drop the subject. *Drop the subject* means that even if you want to know the answer, you stop talking about it because the other person doesn't know the answer or is mad at you for asking too many questions.

Today I don't want Dad to get mad. I want him to finish his research. Because then we can talk about getting a dog.

SIX

OUT THE WINDOW, I SEE MR. JACKSON shuffling back into his house with his golden retriever, Oggie. He is holding a poop bag. That means Oggie must have just finished his pooping and peeing business—time for me to take him for another walk.

"I'm taking *parathas* for Mr. Jackson," I tell Dad as I wrap a few in aluminum foil.

"Have fun with Oggie," he says. I didn't mention Oggie, so how does Dad know what I want to do? Dad's smart like that.

Before I even get to Mr. Jackson's front door, Oggie starts to bark and wag his tail. His nose is pressed against the window. He's seven years old, and we've been friends for a long time.

Mr. Jackson peers through the window, too. He squints, and the lines on his forehead look like crinkled tissue paper. He's kind of cranky, but I don't mind. Mr. Jackson's door is always unlocked, so I walk in. Oggie jumps on me. I have to keep my hand up so he doesn't grab the *parathas*.

"Mr. Jackson, I brought you potato pancakes," I say. Mr. Jackson calls *parathas* potato pancakes.

"Thanks, Suenil. Put 'em on the table, will ya?"

"Sure."

Mr. Jackson mixes Sunil and me up. It's not his fault. It just happens.

Oggie, with his floppy ears and cocoa-brown eyes, follows me into the kitchen.

Oggie barks. He wants yummy *parathas*. But I'm not supposed to give him any.

I make Oggie sit, turn around, and jump up. Then I reward him with a chewy treat.

Oggie puts his paws down on the floor and stretches in front of me.

"Mr. Jackson, may I take Oggie for a walk?" I ask.

No answer.

Mr. Jackson's head has flopped to one side. The voices coming out of the TV can't cover up his snoring.

I ask louder. "MR. JACKSON, MAY I TAKE OGGIE FOR A WALK?"

Mr. Jackson jerks awake. "Who's that? What happened?" He wipes one side of his mouth, which is wet and sticky with his drool.

So I ask for the third time. He waves his hand. "Stay on our cul-de-sac."

"Yup." I put the leash on Oggie before going out.

A cul-de-sac is a street that is curved like a letter *C*. That's why the word *cul-de-sac* starts and ends with *C*. You can only go in and out of it from the open part of the *C*.

I like our cul-de-sac a lot, except when there're certain people on it. Then I feel trapped.

Oggie and I go around twice, and then I see Jenna's brother, Danny Means. He is one of those "certain people." I cross over to avoid him.

He's full of bad habits. I don't worry about

picking up germs from someone. I worry about picking up bad habits. You can wash hands, take a shower, or throw your clothes in the laundry to get rid of germs, but you can't wash off the habits you pick up from someone.

Last Wednesday when I got on the school bus, Danny was already sitting down. "Here comes Eye-shan, the ant," he teased.

Danny calls me *Eye-shan* because he knows it bugs me.

"You're jealous because my ant project won," I said.

"Oh yeah?" He stuck out his leg just as I walked past him. I tripped. Luckily, I landed on him.

"Take your icky ant farm off of me." Then he tried to scare me. "Grrrrr." He sounded like a lion with a turtle stuck in its throat.

"Danny, behave yourself," the driver hollered.

I sat behind Danny.

I unscrewed the cover and peeked inside the ant farm to check on them. A few ants escaped. They climbed on the seat in front, and from there, they climbed onto Danny's neck. It was fun to watch the ants scale a giant mountain—which was really Danny's neck and back, but the ants didn't know that. It was a great adventure for them.

When we got off the bus, I said, "Danny, thanks for letting my ants ride on your back."

"What ants?" he asked. Then he saw a couple of them on his hands. He got busy picking the ants off of his hand.

"See ya later," I said.

As I ran home, he shouted a string of words at me.

Later, when Sunil and I fought, I threw the same string of words at him. I got a time-out for, like, forever.

I can't repeat those words, because I'm not allowed to say them. So I better not. It'd be dumb to get in trouble for the same old thing. Plus, if I repeat Danny's bad old words again and again, they'll become mine. I don't want that. It's better if Danny keeps them.

If I get in trouble now, it'll be for something fresh and unchewed. And I won't mind that one little bit.

"Hey, Eye-shan," Danny shouts. His muddy brown hair is uncombed and the cowlick is sticking up.

I ignore him.

"Saw Sunil this morning—in his Wimpy Kid pajamas. Wait until everyone at school finds out." Danny's grin is evil.

Oops! Sunil is in a boatload of trouble. "Who cares? We're moving this weekend," I say.

"Where?"

I think of an alphabetized list of countries. Sunil knows all of them because he's a fabulous rememberer like that. But I only know the countries that start with A and B. The first one is Afghanistan. There's a war going on in Afghanistan, so Danny wouldn't believe we're moving there. Second on the list is Albania.

"Albania."

He hurries over. "Really? My grandmother is from Albania. She's visiting. Come meet her."

Oh boy. Of all the countries in the world, Danny's grandmother has to be from Albania! And she has to be visiting Danny—at this moment.

I want to be with Oggie, not Danny. "You're not a dog," I say.

He jabs my shoulder. "Why don't you want to meet my grandmother, Eye-shan?"

From the corner of my eye, I see a car turn onto our street. It's Mom. I feel brave. "If I'm Eye-shan, you're Danny Meany with a cowlick."

"Hey! Watch what you're . . ."

Mom drives by. I wave. Danny scowls. Then he waves, too, because she's his doctor. Maybe

he's afraid if he doesn't wave, she'd stick him
with an extra shot. Oggie and I escape to Mr.
Jackson's house.

"Thanks," I say to Mr. Jackson as I take off
Oggie's leash.

"Thank your mother for the potato pancakes. Come over anytime." He smiles. He gets more crinkly but less cranky when he smiles.

"Sure." I dash back out.

Zoom.

Oops! I forgot to close the door behind me, and Oggie runs out into the front yard.

"Get back, Oggie!" I holler. He runs up our driveway and heads straight for Mom. She's carrying two bags of groceries.

"Eeeeshan, take Oggie! Take him away," Mom yells.

"He won't bite you," I say.

Oggie leaps up on her.

"Arragh," goes Mom.

Splat goes a watermelon from her grocery bag.

Chomp, chomp, chomp, goes Oggie.

Mom escapes inside the house. I run back to Mr. Jackson's house and grab Oggie's leash.

Danny walks up. "You're in trouble. Wait until I tell this story, Eye-shan." Danny has the same evil grin on his face as before.

"Who cares? We're moving to Algeria." I say as I walk Oggie back up to Mr. Jackson's house.

"I thought it was Albania."

"Maybe you're getting Albania and Algeria mixed up?" I ask.

Mr. Jackson stands in the doorway. I hand him Oggie with leash and all.

He scowls. He is super-cranky-crinkly now. "You're not Sunil. You're the little rascal."

For once, why does Mr. Jackson have to figure out who I am?

Mom comes out to unload the rest of the groceries. Danny disappears, and I clean up the watermelon mess.

When I go in through the laundry room, I overhear Dad. "Ishan wants a dog real bad."

"He's not getting one," Mom says.

It's better to stay away from the mad alpha dog, Mom. I wash my hands and dash straight for the play set in the backyard.

It's my office. I'm there a lot when I'm not at my real office at school. My brain likes my play office better because, here, it can go where it wants to go.

Today, it's not happy.

It's empty and sad—like a swing without a kid.

SEVEN

THAT AFTERNOON SUNIL GOES TO HIS
friend Jack's house for a sleepover and I call
Alex over to play.

"My mom says I can only come for an hour,"
Alex says.

"Why?"

I can hear him asking his mom. Then she
gets on the phone. "Ishan, Alex has to clean up
his room."

"Okay, Mrs. O'Conner. Thank you," I say.

If Mom is an alpha dog, Alex's mom is a

super-alpha dog. Even *I'm* afraid of her, and I'm not even in her pack.

"What do you want to do?" I ask as soon as Alex arrives.

"Let's go to your backyard office," he says.

"Good idea. That way we won't have to deal with Danny or Jenna."

We flop onto the seesaw. Alex has red hair and green eyes, but we're the same size. So when he pushes his feet against the ground, he goes up and I come down.

"I'm never going to get a dog, and now Mr. Jackson won't let me play with Oggie," I tell Alex.

He looks at me like I'm the saddest thing he has ever seen. And I am.

We take turns going up and down, up and down.

Even with my best friend, I feel sad. I must have real bad CDS.

"Look at that cool butterfly," Alex says,

pointing behind me.

We hop off the seesaw. I'm not pink-and-purple-butterfly crazy, but this one is black. Cool! I grab my bug-catcher from the laundry room. The butterfly flutters about in the garden, and we flutter after it. It escapes us.

"Let's not try to catch it," Alex says.

We're huffy-breath, so I agree. "Let it calm down."

The butterfly settles on a parsley plant. I like the way it just sits there. On its wings, there are two rows of orangey-yellow dots.

"That's a black swallowtail," I say.

"Yup. It likes parsley." Alex is into bugs like I am. He's not an artist, though.

"Maybe we'll see cocoons later in the summer. I'll check every day and call you if I see one," I tell him.

"Cool. Then we can watch it turn into a butterfly."

The swallowtail takes off into the woods

behind my house. Alex and I chase it, but it disappears.

It starts to sprinkle, and we catch some raindrops on our tongues before going in for snacks.

I offer Alex my *paratha*, but he wants chocolate-chip cookies and milk. I eat the same thing because I want to give him company.

By the time Alex goes home, I don't feel sick. Maybe Dad was right. Cookies are good for CDS. And friends are even better.

EIGHT

IN THE EVENING WE GO TO A PARTY.

Indian parties are like my paintings—wild, colorful, and with very few rules.

It's in a big room at the community center. As soon as I open the door, the spicy smell makes me hungry. Inside, everyone is talking, laughing, and eating. Some of them are even talking with their mouths full.

All the people here are like us: *desis*, or Indian-Americans. I call *desi* grown-ups uncles and aunties.

I have too many uncles and aunties. I'm glad I don't have to remember their names. Otherwise it'd be like playing a gigantic memory game, trying to match their faces with their names.

It's someone's anniversary, so everything is extrasparkly. I snip-snap through a bunch of scented aunties. *Swish-swoosh, swish-swoosh,* their colorful saris sing. An auntie wearing a purple sari stops me. "Ishan, *beta,* can you get me some *pani,* please?" This auntie always carries an invisible purse stuffed with chores. Now she hands me one like a piece of candy.

"Sure." I get Chore-Auntie her water.

She ruffles my hair. "Thank you, *beta.*"

"You're welcome, Auntie," I reply politely, because when you call someone *auntie,* you have to be polite.

On my way to the drink table, I pick up a handful of spicy cashews.

My friends Atman and Mayank are chugging

soda with Rasik. Everyone calls him Rick. I met him last week, so I guess he's my friend, too. I pour myself an orange soda.

Yummy!

"Hey, Ishan, try this yellow one," Atman says.

After the yellow soda, I drink a clear soda and then two kinds of brown soda. Then we have a burping contest. I make five real and five fake burps. Atman wins with fifteen burps, but I don't know how many are real. Rick has only three. Then Mayank's burps turn into hiccups.

Atman says, "Eat sugar to get rid of hiccups."

The sugar is by the tea, but too many uncles are hanging out there.

"Let's find desserts. They're full of sugar," I say.

We sneak into the kitchen. No sweets there.

"Maybe they're in this closet," I say as I push open a door.

It's not a closet but an art room filled with

markers and papers. There are pictures taped on the walls. "Look. There," Atman says.

Three trays covered with foil are in a corner. I lift up one end of the foil and find the sweets. Atman rips open a pack of paper plates. We each grab a plate and pile it with sweets. We settle at an art table.

"We're going to get a puppy," I announce as I eat pretzel-like *jalebis*.

"Aren't your parents afraid of dogs? Mine are," Atman says.

I try not to think about Mom, Oggie, and the watermelon mess. "I'm working on that part."

Rick rolls his eyes. "You can have an imaginary dog," Rick says as if he is the boss of my imagination.

"I feel—*urp*—sick," Mayank says. Maybe Rick's rolling eyes made him sick.

"You ate one *jalebi*," Atman says. "You have to eat at least three to get rid of your hiccups."

While we eat, I stare at the sculpture on the table. It's made of twigs, pasta, and beans. Maybe it's three men playing basketball, or a woman carrying a pot of water on her head while bicycling, or a German shepherd with a bumblebee balanced on its long snout.

It inspires me.

Inspire means when someone does something and you want to do the same. Like when the sun paints the sky red or Superman flies, and you want to paint and fly. Now I want to make something.

I cut strips out of black paper and line them on the table.

"What are those?" Mayank asks.

"Train tracks."

I open a tray.

Rick jumps up. "These sweets are not for you to play with."

I point at the *jalebis*. "Who wants to eat things right out of a foil tray? Boring!"

"You'll get in trouble."

"And you won't for scarfing down five *jalebis* and three *laddus*?" Atman asks.

Rick grabs his half-eaten *laddu* and skedaddles out the door.

To *skedaddle* means to get scared and take off.

"I'll be right back," I say and follow him into the hall.

Rick is in the food line, so I budge in front of him. I get some rice, a dab of yogurt, and some okra in a bowl. I return quickly. With the back of the spoon, I squash the rice, okra, and yogurt and make a paste. I put a dab on a round *laddu* and place it on the track.

The glue needs to be stickier.

On one of the shelves, there're five bottles of glue. It says "water-soluble and nontoxic." *Nontoxic* means it won't make you terribly sick and kill you. It's the same kind I ate once when I was four, so I know it doesn't taste too bad. And it really is nontoxic because I'm still alive.

I squeeze some in the okra-rice-yogurt glue.
Now I have new, improved glue.

I stick four *laddus* on the track. They are four wheels.

I put the coconut bars on top of the wheels to make a flatbed train.

"I'm going to make an engine," Atman says.

I pass him the black paper. He knows what to do with it. Our mothers have been friends forever. That means Atman and I were friends before we were even born. That's why we understand each other without talking.

Atman grabs a few more coconut bars. He puts one on the paper and traces it. Then he cuts several pieces. He sticks them on the bar.

While he makes the engine, Mayank and I break off a few *jalebis*. From the broken-off parts we make lions, giraffes, kangaroos, and other animals. We use the curly pieces of *jalebis* to make tails.

Still, we end up with extra pieces of *jalebis*.

It's not good to waste food. Out of black paper, I cut out a butterfly. Then I stick on rounds of *jalebis* to make two rows of orangey spots.

It turns into a swallowtail!

"Let's add more butterflies and some earthworms," Mayank says.

So we do. Our earthworms are beady and orange. I bet Jenna would like these better than one of the smooth brown ones I hung from my wrist to her wrist this morning.

We load the train with animals, and Atman attaches the engine.

"Mayank, your hiccups are gone!" I say.

"And I didn't eat more sweets."

"Train-making worked for hiccups," Atman says.

Finally, we're ready for food.

When we get to the naan tray, I whisper, "Pick extras to make a tunnel."

We sneak back into the art room. We nibble on the naan until they look like arches. Then we stick them together to make a tunnel.

"I'll get a camera from my dad to take pictures," Mayank says, and runs out. Atman follows him.

An uncle walks in.

Oh no! I'm solo.

NINE

I DUCK UNDER THE TABLE. Uncle's eyes turn as round as *parathas* when he sees the sculpture.

"Who-why-what's this?" he stutters.

"A train." Oops! I should've stayed *choop*.

He bends down. I'm eye to eye with him. He asks, "Who are your parents?"

Behind him I can see Atman and Mayank open the door. I don't want them to be trapped like me. So I shake my head and sing, "Go, go, go out of here, merrily, merrily, merrily to the party." It doesn't sound like "Row, row, row your boat," but it doesn't matter, as long as my friends understand what I'm trying to say.

"You're an orphan?" Uncle asks. He seems really annoyed. I guess he didn't like my singing.

Atman points at himself and Mayank as if to say, "Should we get out of here?"

I nod.

They leave.

"If you're an orphan, who takes care of you?" Uncle-in-My-Face asks.

So this is a trick question. Once I tell him Nilesh and Gauri Mehra, he'll know I'm not an orphan. I say, "Shiva and Parvati."

I've never met Shiva and Parvati, but Mom has told me stories about them. They are a god and a goddess. I've seen their statues in temples, so Uncle-in-My-Face must know them, too. Plus, like Dad and Mom, Shiva and Parvati have two sons, Kartik and Ganesh.

Uncle is confused. "Who?" He huffs out the door.

I run to the bathroom because I have to emergency-pee.

Five minutes later, I hear, "Ishan, are you in there?" It's not Shiva. It's my very own dad.

"No." Oops! He knows my voice.

"Come out. Right now," Dad says.

He marches me to the art room.

Dad asks, "Did you make this, this—"

I help him. "A dessert train. For the celebration."

"Wasn't it enough that you made Mom drop the watermelon this morning?" Dad asks, pointing at me.

Mom walks in. When she sees my artwork her hand flies to her mouth. "Ishan! Tell me you didn't do this!"

"I did," I say in my tiny voice.

"Where do you get such crazy ideas?"

I want to tell her they're my very own

because it's good to have original ideas.

Suddenly, *whoosh!* The door opens, and a planeload of uncles, aunties, and kids spill into the room.

Chore-Auntie stands by the door. "What's going on?"

Dad drags me to her and an uncle. I have to look way up because his turban makes him extra-tall. "Show Auntie what you did and apologize," Dad says.

Everyone steps aside.

I stand in front of the sculpture. "I shouldn't have made this dessert train. I'm sorry," I say.

Then I'm *choop*.

Everyone's *choop*.

I stare at my feet. Then I stare at the other people's feet because how long can you stare at your own feet? An itch crawls up my leg.

Chore-Auntie clears her throat. "It's quite lovely. Very creative," she chirps. "Don't you think so?" she asks Turbaned-Uncle.

I look up.

His lips spread out very slowly like the last of toothpaste from a tube. "Yes."

"We love our anniversary dessert train. Don't we?" she asks him.

Turbaned-Uncle's jaw tightens. But he nods.

I didn't know it was Chore-Auntie and Turbaned-Uncle's anniversary. She starts clapping. He starts clapping. Then everyone starts clapping except Mom, Dad, and Uncle-in-My-Face.

Uncle-in-My-Face is scowling. Boy, am I glad it's not his anniversary party!

"Let's take some pictures," Chore-Anniversary-Auntie booms.

Mayank's dad wiggles his way from behind with his camera.

"Stand by your train, Ishan. You're the artist," he says.

"Atman and Mayank helped, too," I say.

"Get in the picture," Chore-Anniversary-Auntie tells them.

Rick shoves himself between Atman and Mayank.

"You didn't do anything," Atman tells Rick.

"You ran away, scaredy-cat," Mayank hisses.

I smile because Mayank's dad is clicking away.

After the pictures, I hold the plate while Mom slides one dessert cart on the plate. I present it to Turbaned-Uncle and Chore-Auntie. "Happy anniversary!"

He takes a bar and a giraffe *jalebi*. She takes a *laddu* and an orange earthworm.

She pinches my cheeks and says, "You are a big *badmash*."

Badmash means *rascal*.

Mom sighs. "Tell me about it!"

Chore-Auntie takes a bite of *laddu*.

"What about the glue?" Atman whispers to me.

"A little glue won't kill such a big auntie."

"Very good *laddu*," she says.

"The glue made it yummier," I tell Atman.

"Time to go home," Mom says.

"Why? Everyone's still partying."

"But we're done, young man," Dad says.

Before Dad starts the car, he turns around. "Ishan, when we get home you'll go straight to your room and think about what you did."

"But Auntie liked my sculpture."

"Do you think Auntie wanted all the desserts made into a train? Do you think people enjoyed eating stuff that you and your friends played with?" Mom asks.

"But why did she clap?"

"What choice did she have?" Mom says. "I feel awful."

My brain starts thinking. Maybe Auntie was trapped into clapping because we had already made our sculpture and there was nothing else she could do.

Suddenly, I also feel awful.

TEN

"DAD THINKS I HAVE CDS," I TELL SUNIL when he gets home Sunday.

Sunil empties his bag and throws the dirty laundry down the chute. "What's CDS?"

"Duh! Canine Deficiency Syndrome."

He laughs. "You ignorant little bug-lover! *Canine* means *dog*. Dad was making fun of you."

"So what? If we can get a puppy out of my CDS, I don't care if it's a fake disease and if people laugh about it."

He stops laughing. "You know Mom doesn't want a dog," he says as he plops onto his bed.

"Mom has veto power. It's a special power because she's our mom."

"Then doesn't Dad have ditto power because he's our dad?" I make a face at him.

"Veto, not ditto," he snorts as he picks up a book.

"I know that. *Ditto* means the same power."

"Whatever. We're never getting a dog," he says.

I want Sunil to be wrong.

I've got to change Mom's mind.

Last month we saw *The Lion King* in Madison. There were no real lions in it, but actors dressed as lions. A kid who acted as Simba had a tail and roared ferociously. I get an idea.

I check on my family. Mom is gardening. Dad and Sunil are going out.

As soon as they leave, I get to work.

I gather up the magazines from the coffee table and take them to my room. I cut out pictures of dogs. I also cut out two pictures of cats. I don't want a cat for a pet, but these two are cute and not scary like Andrew's cat, Tiger. I find sturdy tape in one of the drawers in the laundry room.

There are fourteen family pictures along the wall going down the stairs. I tape the dog and cat pictures between them. The wall has a fresh-painty smell because they were painted the color of watermelon only two weeks ago.

When I'm done, I wash my hands with soap and water. I think of how responsible I am and it makes me feel so good, I want to sing.

I pull out a pair of Sunil's old sweatpants from my clothes pile. I have inherited them, which means I get to wear them after he has worn them for the millionth time. On top of being old, they are ugly. I cut a hole in them so that when I pull them up, there is a big opening in the back where my tail should be.

I grab Mom's purple-and-white scarf with

tassels at the ends. It's Mom-cheek smooth and
not Dad-stubbly-cheek scratchy. I tie it around
my waist and pass one end through the hole.

When I go downstairs, I hear voices coming
out of the kitchen.

I hide in the pantry.

I wait.

And wait.

"Ishan Nilesh Mehra!" Mom screams.
"You've gone too far!"

Yes. I've turned from a kid into a dog.

I come out on my hands and knees.

Dad and Sunil come, too. Mom is at the
bottom of the steps holding on to the railing.
Her eyes are wide.

"Woof, woof," I say.

"What have you done, young man?" Dad
asks, pointing at the pictures.

Uh-oh, now Dad's mad.

But I'm a dog, so I act like one. I roll on the
floor.

Mom pulls on one of the dog pictures. It's stuck solid. "You've ruined the wall."

"Woof, woof-woof." It means, "Mom, it looks great with dogs and cats."

Mom doesn't understand dog language. She plops down on the stair.

I give Mom two quick licks.

"Stop it!" Mom wipes her cheek. Then she runs to the bathroom to wash her hands and maybe her face.

Dad bends down. We're eye to eye. "What was that, young man?"

"Dog kisses," Sunil says.

"Smartypants!" I mumble, even though I'm a dog.

Dad's eyebrows go all zigzaggy again. He pulls me up by my front paws.

"Wooooo-woof," I complain.

"My scarf!" Mom yanks off my tail.

"Ouch!" I shout. "You ripped off my tail." Now I'm just a kid with a hole in my pants.

"Where do you get these crazy ideas from?" Mom asks.

I shrug my shoulders because I don't know where the ideas come from. Maybe there is a bucket filled with ideas in everyone's head.

"Mom asked you a question, Ishan," Dad reminds me.

Most of the time, Mom and Dad want me to be *choop*, so why can't they let me be quiet now? "Idea-bucket," I say.

"You make no sense," Sunil says.

"It's because your idea-bucket is different from mine," I say.

"Never mind. Sunil," Mom says, "let's get some plants."

"Can I come?" I ask.

"Sorry, you have to clean up the wall first." Mom turns to Dad. "Keep an eye on him."

"I'll make sure he does a good job," Dad says.

While I clean, Dad watches golf. Not fair. Everyone's having fun but me.

I tear off the pieces of tape. Some are stubborn. They stick to the wall like Sunil sticks to the rules. I yank them off.

Done.

But now the wall is speckled because the paint is missing in some spots.

Wouldn't Mom be happy if I painted the wall? I peek in the family room. Dad's snoozing while golf is playing. I tiptoe down to the basement where we keep the paints.

There are five paint cans. I carry them up.

Dad and Mom use brushes to spread tomato sauce on pizza or honey on pastries. They keep them in the kitchen. I'm in luck because the second drawer I open has three different-size brushes.

Next I take down all the family pictures and stack them on the side. I spread a rag on the floor to catch the drips. I'm careful like that.

I have blue, pink, yellow, green, and orange colored paints. Now I can turn the wall into a painting. Mom and Dad always hang my artwork on the refrigerator. If I paint the wall, they won't have to worry about hanging my artwork anymore.

Mom loves gardens. I'll make her one.

I'm busy making colorful flowers and butterflies. I use a thick brush for a fat blob of color and a slim one for a skinny dab of color. I paint ants on peonies, a bee on a daisy, and a spider hanging from a shrub. When I finish, it looks awesome, like some painting at the Art Institute of Chicago.

I cover up the cans, take them back to the basement, and put the rag and brushes in the laundry room sink.

"Did you finish cleaning?" Dad hollers.

"Yup. Washing my hands."

Dad watches golf, and I think of what I can do next.

Before I can pull out an idea from my idea-bucket, Mom and Sunil return.

"Did you clean up?" Mom asks.

"Yup. And more."

"Oh no, what did you do?" Mom says, as if I would do something terrible.

When Mom sees the wall, she is speechless. Sunil and Dad are speechless, too.

"You're supposed to keep an eye on Ishan. Since you didn't, you fix it," Mom says to Dad.

"I'm sorry. I fell asleep. I'll repaint it tomorrow."

"Why? Doesn't it look great?" I ask.

"No. You do not paint the wall," Dad says.

Why do we have wall paint if we aren't supposed to paint walls? I want to ask. But I don't because Dad is frowning.

"Our cul-de-sac meeting is in ten minutes," Mom says. "Ishan Nilesh Mehra, during the meeting, stay in the backyard. Remember, you're not allowed in the house or to go out of the yard."

"Tonight we'll decide on your punishment," Dad says.

"This meeting could take forever."

"Then stay there forever, young man," Dad says.

If I stay out forever, then I'm never coming in. It means I'm never getting punished. I don't tell Dad that. He'll figure it out someday.

ELEVEN

BORED.

That's what I am sitting on the seesaw. If I had a dog, I could teach him tricks, we could play Frisbee, we could race each other.

A cardinal sits on the evergreen and sings, *what-cheer*, *what-cheer*. I answer it, "Spring-cheer, spring-cheer." So it knows it is springtime.

I yawn. Then I yawn as loudly as I can to scare all the other yawns that are crowding my mouth.

A bumblebee lands on an apple blossom. Good choice, bumblebee. I run in and grab my binoculars from the laundry room. I'm not allowed in, so I make sure no one sees me. That way, I'm trouble-free.

I get back on the seesaw. It is fun to look at the bumblebee's soft hair through my binoculars. This one is black and yellow.

Sunil comes out. He brings down the seesaw. Sunil is heavier than me, so when he gets on, he stays at the bottom and I hang at the top.

"How are we going to get a dog if you keep messing up?" he asks.

I look at him through the binoculars. "So? You got a better idea?"

"Yes, but I need your cooperation," he says.

Sunil likes to use big gobbledygook words like *cooperation*. It means working together.

"Not happening," I say.

We're both *choop*.

Then my mind thinks, it's already Sunday. Mom and Dad are both mad at me. So Sunil's the only one on my side. Maybe I should listen to him.

"I'll cooperate," I tell Sunil.

"Let's make a plan," he says. He pulls from his pocket a tiny notebook with a tiny pencil.

He starts writing.

"Hey, you said we were going to cooperate," I remind him.

"*Choop!*" When Sunil tells me to be *choop*, it means shut up.

I'm stuck at the top of the seesaw, so I can't even get off.

Finally he reads his ideas: "Take our shoes off in the mudroom so Mom knows we'll keep the carpets clean when we have a dog. Talk more in Hindi at home to make Mom happy."

"Wait!" I say. "No shoes in the house is a *desi* rule. I'm good at taking off my shoes except when I'm not. Like when I'm playing in the backyard and sneak in to grab some gummy bears or my binoculars. Other times, I forget I'm even wearing shoes, so I don't remember to take them off."

"You're not allowed to forget," Sunil says, like he's the boss of my world. "What about the Hindi idea?"

Every day, Mom wants us to talk in Hindi for half an hour. That way, Mom says, we won't miss out on Hindi. Our parents talk in Hindi, watch Hindi movies, and listen to Hindi songs. Hindi is like the extra refrigerator sitting in our basement.

At least our refrigerator stays at home when we go out. Hindi follows us to Indian parties. "*Kaise ho, beta?*" the uncles and aunties ask us in Hindi. Even if we want to, we can't miss it. Don't you have to be away from something to miss it? It is like missing a person while they're staring at you.

"Mom and Dad know English, so why do we

have to speak in Hindi?" I ask.

Sunil bats at a bumblebee. "To get out of trouble. Mom called you by your first, middle, and last names. She's real mad at you."

"So what? Ishan Nilesh Mehra is my name."

He shakes his head. "You always make mischief. Then you get caught. That's no—"

"Hey, once I scrubbed my potty chair with your Cookie Monster toothbrush. And I never got caught," I say.

"What?" Sunil spits out a blob. It looks huge through the binoculars.

"Why are you spitting now? It was a long time ago."

Sunil is as red as a baby's diaper-rashed butt. "You don't deserve a dog. I hope you never get one. I'm going in." His voice is more screechy than his violin.

"Get off slowly, please," I say.

I'm in "the nick of time," as Mr. Jackson would say. Sunil gets off the seesaw slowly.

Even though he's mad, Sunil would never crash me. He's a good brother like that.

"Sorry about the toothbrush." Then I remind him. "Sunil, if I don't get a dog, you won't get one either."

"I don't want to see a dog in our house." He stomps away.

I can't follow him because I'm not allowed in the house.

TWELVE

I SPY ON THE MEETING.

Through the binoculars, I watch people sitting, talking, eating. Danny's parents and his Albanian grandma are there, too.

Yikes!

Mom waves. I bet she's checking up on me. I wave back and throw her a grin.

Why isn't Mr. Jackson at the meeting? I wonder.

I creep closer to his house and look through my binoculars. Inside, I see the nap-chair and the TV, but I don't see Mr. Jackson.

Woof, woof!

Oggie is at the kitchen window.

"Oggie, stop barking," I say.

He keeps on barking. Maybe he can't hear me. Why doesn't Mr. Jackson tell him to be quiet?

Oggie and I are face-to-face, kind of, except that there's a yard, fence, and window in the middle.

Oggie is still barking.

He looks scared and his body is tense. His tail is stiff.

"Oggie, what's the matter?" I ask.

He raises his head up a bit and barks. It sounds like a cry.

I run in the house. "Dad, Oggie's—"

"Wait. Meeting is almost done," Dad says.

I rush back out.

What if something happened to Mr. Jackson?

I must check. But if I leave the backyard, Mom will get mad.

Oggie's bark gets louder.

Mom and Dad are already mad. Even Sunil's mad.

Plus this is an emergency. That means no dillydallying.

I hang the binoculars on the fence and sprint to Mr. Jackson's house.

THIRTEEN

WHEN I OPEN THE DOOR, OGGIE'S RIGHT there. "Mr. Jackson?" I call.

No answer.

Oggie runs. I follow him. Mr. Jackson is on the kitchen floor!

I touch his hand. "Mr. Jackson?"

He doesn't answer. I call 9-1-1.

"My neighbor is sick," I tell the person who answers the phone.

"Hang on the line until the ambulance arrives," the 9-1-1 person tells me. He already knows Mr. Jackson's address!

I take the phone and run to our house. "Mom, Mr. Jackson has fainted."

"Oh no!" Mom follows me.

"I already called 9-1-1," I tell her on the way to Mr. Jackson's.

"Good!"

While Mom checks Mr. Jackson, I offer Oggie a treat. He doesn't want it. I talk to him so he knows what's going on. "Oggie, my mom's checking Mr. Jackson's pulse. She won't hurt him. Everything will be fine."

Mr. Jackson opens his eyes. "How're you feeling?" Mom asks him.

His lips flutter, but nothing comes out.

Dad and Sunil rush in with Mom's stethoscope.

"Your heart sounds fine. Does anything hurt, John?" Mom asks.

"Can't tell for sure. I was going to come over for the meeting but felt worn out. I rested a bit. Then tried to put on . . ." He closes his eyes.

"Just rest," Mom says.

I scratch Oggie under the chin. "Didn't I tell you Mr. Jackson is fine, Oggie?"

He gives me a kiss.

And then the siren blares. Oggie leaps up. "The ambulance is here," I tell the 9-1-1 person before hanging up. Sunil and I take Oggie to Mr. Jackson's bedroom and close the door.

We can't hear what people are saying because Oggie is barking away like that's his only business.

Finally it's quiet. We come out.

"They took Mr. Jackson to the hospital to run some tests. Mom followed them," Dad says.

"Will he be okay?" Sunil asks.

"He was probably tired—Mom thinks that's why he fainted. But once they run the tests, we'll know for sure."

"Hear that, Oggie?" I ask.

He wags his tail. He understands.

"Let's lock up and go home with Oggie," Dad says.

"But Mom's scared of Oggie," Sunil says.

"Mom will be fine if you two take care of him."

"I can't believe you're coming home with

us," I whisper to Oggie. He wags his I-am-happy tail. We gather up his dog dishes, food, and treats. I pick up an old shirt of Mr. Jackson's, too.

"Sunil, now there's a dog in our house," I say when we get home.

"Oggie doesn't count."

Oggie licks my nose. "He's a dog. And he's in our home. So it counts."

"You'll have to take Oggie back when Mr. Jackson comes home."

"By that time, Mom will want a dog of our own," I say.

I must make sure that Mom loves Oggie. Which means no dog accidents.

FOURTEEN

"SUNIL, LET'S TAKE OGGIE FOR A WALK,"
I say.

"I have homework."

I leash Oggie.

Sunil gives me a sneaky smile. "You better
carry a poop bag."

I'm not a fan of poop bags or sneaky smiles.

I take a plastic bag and a pair of disposable
gloves Mom keeps for emergencies. I'm hoping
I won't have to use them.

Oggie and I trace our cul-de-sac three times. Oggie pees and finally poops—in Danny Means's yard. I put the gloves on and bend down. As I pick up the poop I hear a chuckle: "Haa, haa, hee, hee."

"Want to see dog poop?" I ask as I swing the bag.

Big mistake.

It isn't Danny. It's Jenna.

"Yuck!" she screams.

Danny yells from his house. "Stop bugging Jenna!"

"She came out. I didn't ask her," I say.

Danny disappears.

"Ishan is a doggie-doo poop-picker," Jenna sings.

"My mom will stick you with three extra shots," I hiss.

Jenna's face falls apart. Mom is her doctor. Once when Mom got a shot ready, Jenna ran out the door, through the waiting room, and clear across the parking lot. So she is plenty afraid of shots. Mom never told me this, but Danny told Sunil and he told me.

"She's not mean like you. She won't," Jenna says.

I pull Oggie's leash.

Danny and his Albanian grandma come out. Double yikes!

"Are you Ishan?" Danny's grandma asks. Her eyes are icy blue and her stare makes me feel as tiny as a bumblebee.

"Yes," I say.

"You painted the wall?"

"Do you want me to paint your walls?" I ask.

"Never mind," she says. "I heard you're moving. Albania or Algeria?"

"Umm . . . both places. I mean first we go to one and then to the other."

"Your parents said you weren't moving."

"They changed their minds? They never want me to have fun," I say.

"You're one of a kind." She starts laughing. "Haa, haa, hee, hee." She sounds just like Jenna. Except she's as wrinkled as Mr. Jackson.

"I've got to take Oggie home," I say.

She puts her hand on my shoulder. "Thanks for calling 9-1-1. You saved dear John's life. Didn't he, Danny?"

"Yes, Grandma," Danny says. He doesn't look like his usual Danny-the-Meany self.

"Take care of that dog," she says.

I nod.

"Good. Let's go in, Danny," she orders.

I tug at Oggie's leash.

"Poop-picker!" Jenna's voice follows me.

FIFTEEN

WHEN MOM COMES HOME, OGGIE WAGS his tail, barks, and jumps on her.

Mom screeches.

I hold on to Oggie. "How's Mr. Jackson?"

"Fine, but they're keeping him overnight. Megan is with him."

Megan is Mr. Jackson's daughter. "Is she going to take Oggie?"

Mom takes off her shoes. "Not tonight."

"Can Oggie sleep with me?" Sunil asks.

Before Mom can answer, I say, "I was the one who heard Oggie's bark and found Mr. Jackson. I want Oggie to sleep in my room."

"But I asked first," Sunil says.

Oggie and I follow Mom and Sunil into the family room.

Dad closes his laptop. "The dog will stay in our room."

"Oggie's upset and he doesn't know you well. Bad idea," I say.

"Ishan's right," Mom says. "And he helped Mr. Jackson, so Oggie should sleep with him."

Sunil shouts. "Not fair! Ishan got there first because he was in the yard. He had time-out. And he broke the rule and went over. Yesterday he crushed garlic with my pencil box. Now it stinks. He even used my Cookie Monster toothbrush to clean his potty. Ishan—"

"Sunil, you make no sense," Mom says as she draws the window blinds shut.

"I do, too. Ask him about the potty."

"We're talking about Oggie and not a potty," Dad says. "Let's deal with one thing at a time."

"Ishan, how did you know something was wrong?" Mom asks.

"Oggie barked and barked. I asked him to be quiet, but he wouldn't." Suddenly, I remember something. "Excuse me," I say. Oggie and I run out, grab my binoculars, drop them in the laundry room, and return as quick as you can say *zip-zoom-za*.

"One of the paramedics said you're a smart boy, Ishan," Mom says.

"Why is he a smart boy? I'm the one who gets all As," Sunil says.

"He called 9-1-1," Mom reminds him.

"If Oggie hadn't barked, I wouldn't have known that Mr. Jackson was in trouble. He's a great dog," I say, patting him.

"Yes," Mom agrees.

"Should we think about getting a dog like Oggie?" I ask.

Mom plops down on the couch. "I need some tea."

How did tea get into our talk?

"I'll make you some," Dad says, and goes into the kitchen.

I let go of Oggie and he tries to jump on Mom.

"Take him," she shouts.

"He wants to be your friend," I tell her.

"None of my friends jump."

I think of all the aunties and uncles. It's better that they don't jump. "Oggie is different."

Mom tries to pat Oggie. He raises his head. Mom pulls back. "He's baring his teeth. He'll bite," she says, tucking her feet under her.

"He won't," Sunil says.

Mom's eyes turn narrow. "Stay away, Oggie."

"Hold your palm out. That's saying hello in dog," I say.

Mom holds her palm out. I hold on to her so she can't pull back when Oggie tries to sniff her. "Now pat him under his chin so he can see what you're doing." I gently scratch Oggie under the chin. "Like this."

Mom does. "He didn't bite!"

Oggie settles down by Mom.

Dad brings in tea. He's puzzled. "What happened in the last five minutes?"

"Mom and Oggie became friends," I tell him.

"I want to become Oggie's friend, too."

"Hold your hand out like this and let Oggie sniff you," she says.

Sunil and I grin at each other.

SIXTEEN

"CAN I ALSO SLEEP IN YOUR ROOM?" SUNIL asks.

"Only if I can come into your room without knocking," I say.

"Okay," Sunil says. He sounds grumpy, like a dog that just lost a bone in a fight.

I spread Mr. Jackson's old shirt for Oggie to lie on. Then I sleep on a sleeping bag next to him. Sunil takes my bed.

Oggie and I are the first ones to wake up. I

change my clothes and take him for a walk. No one else is on the street. Phew!

Oggie stops in front of his house and looks at it with such sad eyes that I tell him, "Come, Oggie. I'll give you a treat."

When we get home I give him a couple of leftover chewy chicken nuggets even though he hasn't had breakfast. I keep my promise so he can trust me.

Then I give him dog chow and fill his water bowl.

I point to the dishes. "Food, Oggie." He doesn't eat. I take a few pieces in my hand and offer it to him. He eats them. So I hand-feed him. "Good boy! Eat your breakfast," I say.

When Mom comes in the kitchen, Oggie runs to her. "Take him away," Mom says.

"Remember, Oggie's your friend. He wants a good-morning pat."

She dumps Cheerios in a bowl. "Maybe later."

"Why later? Don't you wish your friends a good morning as soon as you see them?"

Mom smiles. "Yes."

I pick up a Cheerio from her bowl. "Watch this," I say as I hold it out in my palm. Oggie eats it. "Your turn."

Mom offers a Cheerio, but before Oggie can take it, she tosses it away.

"It's okay. You'll learn," I tell her.

She pours milk in her bowl. "You really like dogs, don't you?"

"I love dogs. I love our dog without even having one."

"Oh, Ishan!" Mom sighs.

"Once we have a dog, you'll love him. You won't be afraid of him because he won't ever hurt you," I say.

"Are you sure?"

"Yes. But you must never pet a strange dog. And never feed a dog chocolate, spinach, onions, or grapes. Those are poisonous for them."

"What about watermelon? Oggie ate that yesterday."

"A little watermelon is fine."

"How come you know all about dogs?" Mom asks.

"I read dog books, I watch dog movies. I even turned myself into a dog yesterday. Remember?"

"How could I forget?" Mom says. She puts a couple of Cheerios on the floor. Oggie eats them and sits down at Mom's feet. Mom moves her hand through Oggie's fur. He likes Mom.

Sunil comes in the kitchen. "Hi, Oggie," he greets the dog before he even says good morning to Mom.

Suddenly, Oggie runs to the door.

From the window, I see Megan walking up. She's here to pick up Oggie.

Before Mom opens the door, Sunil and I race upstairs. Sunil doesn't want Megan to see his Wimpy Kid pajamas. I don't feel like saying good-bye to Oggie.

Sunil runs to his room and closes the door.
Just like I thought: he is going to change out
of his pajamas. I go to my room and wait for
Megan to leave. When I go down Oggie will be
gone, too. I miss him already.

My CDS is making me really sick.

SEVENTEEN

AFTER THE DOOR SHUTS, I STILL HEAR
Oggie's bark. I come bounding down.

Sunil is wrestling with Oggie. "We're
keeping Oggie one more day."

I hug Mom. "You're the best mom in the
whole world."

Dad winks at me. I wink right back.

"Why are you scared of dogs, Mom?" I ask.

"Because there were too many stray dogs
when I was growing up. They lived on the

streets and were dangerous," Mom says. Her eyebrows go up.

"You mean no one fed them and played with them?" I ask.

Mom nods.

"I bet they felt sad. Like I'd feel without you. See how well Oggie behaves? Because he knows Mr. Jackson loves him. Last night I gave him Mr. Jackson's old shirt to make him feel better. I feed Oggie and give him treats and play with him so he knows I love him. If you love a dog, it'll love you right back."

She puts her arm around me. "How did you become so wise?"

"Dogs make me wise. Without them, I'm wild," I tell her.

Mom's eyes twinkle.

"If we get a dog, I'll feed him and take him for a walk every day," Sunil says.

That means he'll have to deal with Danny, Jenna, and their grandma. Phew!

"I can bathe him," Dad says.

"I'll play with him and sleep with him," I say.

"No, he'll sleep with me," Sunil says.

"If you fight, we can't get a dog," Mom says.

"We won't. We promise," Sunil and I both say.

"I guess we can get a dog," Mom says.

"You're the best mom in the whole world!" I tell her again. I also give her a kiss. A regular kiss. Not a doggie one.

EIGHTEEN

"Do you think we should give our dog an Indian name?" Sunil asks.

Sometimes Sunil picks out a great idea from his idea-bucket. "Yes," I say as I play with Oggie. "Mom will like that. And if she likes the dog's name, she'll like the dog."

Sunil grins. "How about Badam, if he's light brown?"

"Danny will split the name: Bad-am, Bad-am."

Sunil shakes his head, slow and sad. "How about Almond?"

"*Almond* is not a Hindi word. *Badam* is."

"Oh!"

"If we get a golden retriever, we could name him Sona because it means *gold*," I say.

"Sona sounds like Sunil. Danny will make fun of me."

"But they're not the same. *Sunil* means deep, dark blue. Not gold."

Sunil looks puzzled because his eyebrows scrunch up.

I'm not puzzled because I'm an artist. I know gold and dark blue aren't alike.

I let Sunil unpuzzle himself while I let my mind play with a bouncy, flouncy puppy named Sona.

It's almost as good as playing with a real one because I almost have my dog.

And right now I also have Oggie.

Yaaaaaay!